THIS NOTEBOOK BELONGS TO

Made in the USA
Monee, IL
04 November 2022

17133461R00056